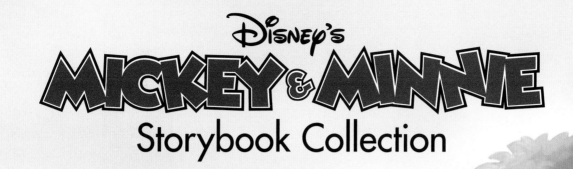

Disney's MICKEY & MINNIE

Storybook Collection

Disney PRESS

Los Angeles · New York

Contents

Disney's
MICKEY & MINNIE

A Sure Cure for the Hiccups

Mickey sighed. He had been hiccupping all morning. And it was very hard to paint shutters with the hiccups! Every time Mickey picked up his brush—

"*Hic!*" His body shook and paint flew everywhere.

Minnie was passing by and noticed that Mickey looked upset. "What's wrong?" she asked.

"Oh, hiya—*hic!*—Minnie," Mickey replied. "It's nothing. *Hic!* I just can't seem—*hic!*—to get rid of these hiccups!"

Minnie invited Mickey next door. Inside, she poured him a glass of water. "Take a tiny sip," Minnie said. "Then count to five and take another sip."

Mickey gave it a try. But the hiccups just kept coming.

"Hmmm," said Minnie. "Try it with your eyes closed."

Mickey closed his eyes and took a sip. "One, two, three, four—*hic!*"

Just then, there was a knock at Minnie's door. Daisy had come over for their daily walk.

"Hiya—*hic!*—Daisy," said Mickey. "*Hic! Hic!*"

"Wow," Daisy said, coming inside. "It sounds like you need my tried-and-true hiccup cure! It may seem silly, but it will take your mind off your hiccups. Just do what I do."

Daisy stood on her tiptoes. Mickey did, too. Daisy twirled out Minnie's front door. Mickey did, too.

Daisy did two high kicks, tap-danced down the front walk, spun around once, and took a bow.

Mickey wasn't sure he could do all that. But he was willing to *try* anything. So he high-kicked, tap-danced, and spun right to Daisy's side.

"Good job, Mickey!" Daisy said. "How are your hiccups?"

Mickey's face brightened. "Hey!" he shouted. "I think they're gone! Thanks, Daisy. You're the—*hic!*" Mickey frowned. "I guess they're not gone after all."

"Hmmm," said Daisy. "Maybe Donald knows a good cure for hiccups. Let's go ask him."

The three friends set out to find Donald. But Minnie and Daisy were much faster than Mickey. When he arrived at Donald's house, they were waiting by the front door.

"Where's Donald?" Mickey asked.

Before Daisy could answer, Donald jumped out at Mickey.

"*Aaaaaaah!*" Mickey cried.

"Sorry, Mickey," Donald said. "Daisy and Minnie said you have the hiccups. I thought maybe I could scare them away."

Minnie, Daisy, and Donald watched Mickey closely. "Did it work?" Minnie asked.

But Mickey just hiccupped again.

"Aw, phooey," Donald said.

Mickey tried everything he could think of to get rid of his hiccups. He stood on his head while saying the alphabet backward. "*Hic!*"

He held his nose and whistled a tune while hopping on one foot. "*Hic!*"

He skipped rope and sang, "M, my name is Mickey—*hic!*—I have a friend named Minnie—*hic!*—and I like mints! *Hic! Hic!*"

Mickey sat down in Donald's hammock and moped. He was starting to feel like he would never get rid of his hiccups. "It's no use," he said to his friends. "I think my hiccups are—*hic!*—here to stay."

Daisy led Minnie and Donald to the side of the yard. The three of them whispered to one another for several minutes. They had to find a way to help Mickey! Finally, Donald rushed inside and returned with a large sack.

Donald reached into the sack and pulled out some blocks. Concentrating hard, he balanced three of them on his bill!

Next Minnie and Daisy pulled two hoops out of the sack. They hung one on each of Donald's arms, and he began to twirl them.

"Okay, Mickey!" Donald said. "Now you try!"

Mickey wanted to try, but all he could do was laugh! "I'm sorry, Donald," he said between giggles. "You just look so . . . silly!"

"Silly?!" Donald said crossly. "You call this silly?"

Mickey just laughed harder.

When he finally stopped laughing, Mickey realized something. His hiccups were gone. He and his friends waited and waited—but not another hiccup came!

"I did it!" Donald cried. "I cured Mickey!"

"You sure did, Donald," Mickey said. "I guess laughter really *is* the best medicine—for hiccups!"

A Surprise for Pluto

One sunny morning, Mickey Mouse looked out the window. "What a beautiful day!" he exclaimed. "This is perfect building weather."

His nephews, Morty and Ferdie, joined him. "What are you going to build, Uncle Mickey?" asked Morty.

Mickey's eyes twinkled. "Oh, I don't know," he said. "Maybe . . . a tree house!"

The boys jumped up and down. "A tree house?" Ferdie said.

"Can we help?" Morty asked.

"You would be great helpers," Mickey replied. "But there will be lots of tools in the yard. It might not be very safe. Why don't you take Pluto to the park instead?"

"Sure, Uncle Mickey!" the boys replied.

With Morty, Ferdie, and Pluto gone, Mickey called his friends.
He told them all about the tree house and asked if they would like
to help.

Soon Minnie, Donald, Daisy, and Goofy arrived in Mickey's yard.

"Building a tree house is a big job," Mickey said. "Maybe we should split up the work."

"Great idea, Mickey," Goofy said.

"Why don't you saw the boards, Goofy," Mickey said. "Then Donald and I can hammer them together."

Minnie showed Mickey a special drawing she had made.

"Good thinking, Minnie!" Mickey said. "That will be one of the most important jobs of all."

Goofy dumped out his toolbox in a corner of the yard. The tools made a big crash—and a big mess! Goofy found what he was looking for and began sawing the boards.

After a few minutes, Minnie walked up to him. "Sorry to bother you, Goofy," she began. "I was wondering if you would cut some boards for me, too."

"Sure!" Goofy said with a grin. "Just tell me what you need."

Over by the big tree, Donald and Mickey worked together to make a rope ladder. When they were finished, Mickey attached the ladder to the thickest branch. He gave the ladder a strong tug. It didn't budge.

"That should do it," Mickey said. "Once we finish building, we can use this ladder to climb into the tree house."

Just then, Goofy brought them a stack of boards. "Here you go!"
he said proudly. "I still have to saw the boards for the roof, but you
can use these for the floor and the walls."

"Thanks, Goofy!" Mickey said.

Mickey and Donald climbed into the tree, pulling the boards
behind them. The sounds of their hammers echoed through the
backyard as the friends started building.

Across the yard, Minnie pulled her hammer out of her tool belt. As she picked up the first board, she realized that she had forgotten something very important.

Minnie hurried over to the big tree. "Do you have any extra nails?" she called up. "I left all of mine at home!"

"I have some," Donald said. He fished a box of nails out of his tool belt and gave them to Minnie.

On the way back to her project, Minnie stopped to see how Daisy was doing.

"Wow, Daisy," Minnie said. "You mixed up a lot of paint!"

Daisy giggled. "I might have mixed a little *too* much," she said. "Do you need any paint for your project?"

"Thanks, Daisy," Minnie said. "That would be great!"

Soon everyone was hard at work.

Buzz-buzz-buzz went the saw.

Bang-bang-bang went the hammers.

Swish-swish-swish went the paintbrushes.

Mickey's backyard was a very busy place!

Later that day, Morty, Ferdie, and Pluto came home from the park. Morty and Ferdie couldn't believe their eyes. "Wow!" the boys cried.

"This is the best tree house ever!" added Ferdie as they scrambled up the rope ladder.

Beneath them, Pluto whined. He couldn't climb the ladder like the others.

Mickey understood right away. "Don't worry, Pluto!" he called.
"Come around to the other side of the tree."

Pluto trotted around the tree and found something that made
his tail wag: a set of stairs that was just his size!

"Minnie made them for you," Mickey explained. "Now come
on up and join the fun!"

Pluto ran up the stairs. It really *was* the best tree house ever!

Disney's MICKEY & MINNIE

Donald Duck
and the Buried Treasure

One afternoon, Donald Duck and his nephews, Huey, Dewey, and Louie, were taking a drive. Soon they found themselves going through a small village near the water. Suddenly, Donald slammed on the brakes.

"What's wrong, Uncle Donald?" asked the boys.

Donald pointed to a sign by a shop.

It said GENUINE PIRATE MAPS 25¢.

"Pirate treasure!" the boys yelled. "Yippee! Can we get a map, Uncle Donald? Please?"

Donald went inside the shop and found the shopkeeper.

"Are you looking for a treasure map?" the shopkeeper asked slyly.

Donald nodded, and the man handed him a map.

Then, because treasure hunters need things besides maps, the shopkeeper sold Donald a shovel, a pickax, a compass, ropes for hauling up the treasure, and sacks for carrying it home. Last of all, he rented Donald the biggest boat at the dock.

In no time, Donald and his nephews were rowing out to the island on the map.

"Look for the forked tree. Take ten paces north, then dig," Donald read.

Donald and his nephews looked around for the tree.

"There it is!" Huey yelled. "Let's go."

At the tree, they took ten paces north and began to dig. But there was no treasure.

They dug ten paces to the west and ten to the east. But still there was no treasure.

Donald was furious. He threw down his shovel and glared at the treasure map. "This map is a fake!" he shouted. "There is no treasure buried on this island. Phooey!"

But his nephews had heard something. "Shhh!" they whispered. "Don't shout, Uncle Donald. You'll scare the ghost away."

Donald blinked. "What ghost?" he asked.

Then Donald heard it, too.

Clank, clank, clank.

"Th-there's no such thing as a ghost," Donald said, his voice shaking.

But his nephews weren't so sure. Slowly they crept up a hill, following the noise.

The boys looked down and saw people digging all over the island. Each had a treasure map!

"I knew it!" Donald yelled. "These maps are fakes! I guess the joke's on us. Okay, boys, let's go home."

At the boat, Donald tried to pull up the anchor. He tugged and tugged, but it wouldn't budge. Finally, with one last pull, the anchor came out of the water—bringing with it a big iron chest!

Donald lifted the pickax. "Stand back, kids!" he cried.

With the first swing, the old lock on the chest snapped. Donald slowly lifted the lid. Inside were hundreds and hundreds of gold and silver coins!

"We found it!" the nephews shouted. "It's real pirate treasure!"

"I knew we would find it!" Donald exclaimed.

Donald quickly rowed back to the mainland. "Just one second, boys," he said as his nephews brought the chest to their car. "There's something I need to do."

Donald walked into the store and dropped a gold coin into the shopkeeper's hand.

"Thanks for the map," he said, and walked back out.

Donald waited outside. A second later, the shop door flew open and the shopkeeper ran out. He had a shovel in one hand and a map in the other.

"They really *are* genuine!" he cried.

Donald and his nephews watched the shopkeeper hop into his boat.

"Good luck!" Donald yelled.

"Happy hunting!" cried Huey, Dewey, and Louie.

The boys waved good-bye, and then they all went home to count their genuine pirate treasure.

Goofy's Pie Shop

"Who wants pie?" Goofy asked.

Minnie and Mickey were at Goofy's house. They had just finished dinner, and it was time for dessert.

"I do!" Mickey said.

Goofy brought a steaming hot blueberry pie to the table.

"Wow, Goofy!" said Minnie. "This looks great! Where did you buy it?"

"I didn't buy it," Goofy answered. "I made it myself!"

Goofy's pie was delicious. The blueberries were bursting with juice, and the crust was perfectly crunchy.

"I had no idea you were such a good cook!" Minnie said as she served herself a second slice.

"You should open a pie shop!" Mickey agreed, helping himself to a third piece.

"Hmmm!" Goofy said. "That *does* sound like fun!"

Goofy didn't waste any time. The next morning he rented an
empty shop on Main Street. It was small, but there was enough
room for a counter and a few tables. Goofy couldn't wait to start
fixing it up.

57

Goofy rolled up his sleeves and got to work. There was so much to do! Finally, his shop was ready. It had new floors, new wallpaper, a new counter, new tables and chairs . . .

There was even a fancy new light!

Goofy thought his pie shop was the most beautiful thing he'd ever seen.

Goofy couldn't wait to show off his shop. And he knew just how to do it. He would invite the whole town to a Grand Opening party.

Goofy stood in front of his new shop and gave an invitation to everyone who walked by. Soon the town was buzzing with the news! Everybody was excited to try Goofy's pies.

Goofy was just handing out his last invitation when Minnie
passed by. "I can't wait for your party!" she told him. "Have you
planned your menu yet?"

"You bet!" Goofy said. "I'm going to make all my favorites . . .
peanut butter and jelly pie, bean pie, grape pie, cheese pie,
vinegar pie, raisin pie, and bacon pie."

Minnie just stared at him. The menu seemed so strange!

"We have to do something, Mickey!" Minnie said later that night. "Goofy is making the strangest pies I've ever heard of. What if no one eats them?"

Mickey looked worried. "We were the ones who told him to open a pie shop," he said. "If it doesn't go well . . ."

"Then it's all our fault!" Minnie finished. "We have to save him!"

Mickey agreed. He rushed off to talk to Goofy about the pies.

Mickey found Goofy at his shop, rolling out piecrusts.

"Hiya, Mickey," Goofy said. "I was just fixing my menu. I thought I had it all worked out, but I was wrong."

Mickey breathed a sigh of relief. "I'm glad to hear—" he started. But Mickey didn't have a chance to finish his sentence.

"I need more kinds of pie," Goofy interrupted. "I'm adding green-tomato pie, shoofly pie, and potato pie."

The day of the party, Minnie visited Goofy in his kitchen. She was still nervous about his menu.

"Won't you please make something normal?" she begged.

Goofy tried to explain. "I don't want to make the same boring pies that everyone always eats," he said. "I want people to be surprised!"

Minnie nodded sadly. Goofy could see that she was still upset. Finally, he agreed to make one apple pie.

Soon the guests arrived. Mickey and Minnie watched nervously as Goofy's guests tried his strange pies. Happy sounds filled the air.

"This potato pie is amazing!" Donald Duck exclaimed.

"Gooseberry! My favorite!" cried Gladstone Gander.

Mickey and Minnie were surprised—Mickey loved the bacon pie and Minnie adored the shoofly pie. They had never been so happy to be wrong!

When the party was over, Mickey and Minnie looked around. There was only one pie left!

"Nobody ate the apple pie!" Minnie said.

"Why don't we eat it?" Mickey said.

"Goofy's probably too full after all those other pies," Minnie answered.

"Actually . . ." Goofy said, "I was so busy serving pie, I forgot to eat any!"

So the three friends sat down to share the plain apple pie.

It was delicious.

Happy Sailing

One lovely summer day, Mickey Mouse asked his girlfriend, Minnie, if she'd like to go for a boat ride.

"I would love to," Minnie said with a smile. "A nice, easy ride sounds like the perfect way to spend the day."

Mickey and Minnie were preparing to set sail when Goofy came running by.

"Hiya, Mickey. Hiya, Minnie," he said, and waved. "What a great day for a boat ride!"

Goofy was so busy looking at Mickey's boat that he didn't see a squirrel crossing his path. He accidentally stepped on its tail.

The squirrel leaped away and landed in the boat.

Mickey and Minnie were so startled that they jumped up, making the boat rock.

Mickey tried to stop the rocking, but he could not. The boat tipped over, sending Mickey and Minnie into the water.

Donald Duck was nearby in his speedboat and saw what had happened. He helped Mickey and Minnie into his boat. "Why don't you ride with me for a while?" he said. "You can take it easy and let the engine do the work."

Mickey and Minnie sat back and relaxed, listening to the happy *putt-putt* of the engine. They had just reached the middle of the lake when the boat's engine suddenly stopped.

"What do we do now?" Minnie asked.

"I have an idea," Donald said. He took off his hat and started to paddle with it.

Mickey and Minnie did the same. Huffing and puffing, they made their way back to shore.

"How about some lunch while we dry off?" Mickey said.

Minnie agreed, and the two were soon relaxing in the sun with hot dogs.

As they were enjoying their lunch, Pluto ran by. When he saw the delicious hot dogs, he decided he wanted one, too. He jumped into Mickey's lap and tried to grab the food.

"Stop it, boy!" cried Mickey.

"Pluto," said Minnie, "if you want a hot dog, we can get you one."

But it was too late. Pluto knocked Mickey and Minnie right into the water!

Mickey and Minnie climbed out of the water and settled on the grass to dry off again. Soon Donald Duck's nephews, Huey, Dewey, and Louie, came by in their sailboat.

"Hey, Mickey," called Dewey. "Would you and Minnie like to borrow our boat and go sailing? There's a good wind today."

"I've always wanted to try sailing!" said Minnie excitedly. "It's supposed to be a lot of fun."

Mickey and Minnie hopped into the triplets' boat and took off.

"Aah, this is the life," Mickey said a few minutes later.

"At last, a nice, easy boat ride," said Minnie.

Just then, the wind stopped blowing.

Mickey and Minnie were stranded again! They tried to paddle with their hands, but it was no use.

Suddenly, Mickey looked up. Goofy and Donald were paddling toward them in rowboats.

"We thought you might need some help," said Donald.

"How about a tow to shore?" Goofy offered.

As the sun began to set over the peaceful lake, Mickey and
Minnie sat back and relaxed. They had finally gotten their nice,
easy boat ride!

Disney's MICKEY & MINNIE

Cowboy Mickey

Mickey Mouse was busily packing his suitcase. He and his friends were going to the Lucky Star Dude Ranch.

Mickey was excited. He had always wanted to learn how to ride a horse.

Just then, Goofy raced into Mickey's room. "I'm all packed!" he shouted. "I'm going to learn how to twirl a lasso so I can perform in the rodeo!"

Goofy couldn't wait to show everyone how well he could ride. The minute they reached the ranch, he hopped onto the first horse he saw. But he jumped onto it backward!

Goofy held on tightly to the horse's tail as it bucked in circles. "What do I do now?" he cried.

Luckily, Minnie had brought a bunch of carrots with her to feed the horses. She held one out to the horse, and he happily trotted over to eat it.

"Whew! That was close!" Goofy gasped. "Thanks for showing up with those carrots, Minnie."

Mickey and his friends went inside to change into their riding clothes.

When they came back out, the owner of the ranch was waiting for them. "It looks like you folks need a few lessons," he said. "I'm Cowboy Bob. Let me show you the right way to ride a horse."

"Hey, this isn't hard at all," bragged Goofy as he trotted along on his horse a few minutes later. "Now I'm ready to learn how to use a lasso!"

The next day, Mickey and Minnie practiced their riding while Goofy practiced with his lasso.

"You're learning fast," Cowboy Bob said to Mickey and Minnie. "I bet you'll both be good enough to perform in the rodeo."

"How about me?" asked Goofy. "Watch how well I twirl this lasso."

Goofy whirled the lasso around and around. But instead of catching a horse, he caught his own foot!

"Whoops!" Goofy cried as he fell down. "I'd better practice some more!"

Finally, the day of the big rodeo arrived. Cowboys from all over gathered to see the show. Inside, Mickey was still asleep! He had forgotten to set his alarm clock!

As the noisy crowd passed by his window, it woke him up.

Mickey looked at the time. He had to hurry!

Mickey quickly got dressed and dashed out the door. He raced across a field, jumped over a fence . . . and landed right on a bucking bronco in the middle of the rodeo!

Everyone cheered as Mickey held tightly to the reins.

"Hey! This is sort of fun!" he cried.

As Mickey waved his hat to the crowd, the announcer cried out, "Mickey Mouse has just broken the ranch record for the longest-ever bronco ride!"

Goofy wanted to show what he could do, too, and tried to lasso the bronco. But instead he lassoed Mickey. "Whoops!" he said with a chuckle.

Later that day, the crowd cheered as Cowboy Bob presented the rodeo ribbons.

Minnie won for taking good care of the horses. Mickey won for his bronco riding. And Goofy won for trying to lasso everything in sight!

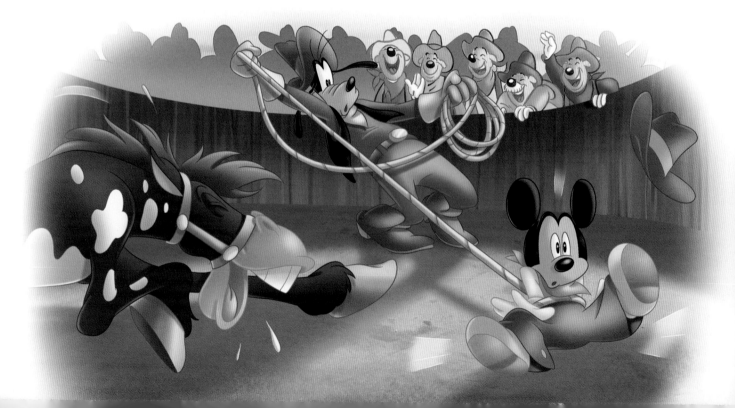

"This has been the most fun I've ever had," Mickey told Minnie later that night. Just then, he spotted an odd shape against the moon. "Look, it's a coyote!" Mickey shouted. "Now I *really* feel like a cowboy."

"Do you want me to lasso him?" asked Goofy.

"No thanks," everyone said with a laugh, and they went back to enjoying the fire.

Donald Duck
and the County Fair

Donald Duck was excited. Daisy had agreed to go with him to the county fair!

Donald puffed out his chest. He couldn't wait to show off for Daisy. He was sure he could ride any ride and win any game.

"What should we do first?" Daisy asked.

"How about the roller coaster?" Donald suggested. "The loop-the-loop. The speed swings. Nothing scares me!"

Daisy peered around the fairground. "Look!" she cried. "The spinning teacups. I love that ride!"

"Hmmm . . ." Donald said. "It looks a little boring, but if that's what you want to do . . ."

Daisy grabbed Donald's hand and pulled him over to a teacup.

The ride started and Daisy took the spinning wheel. The teacup made a lazy circle. Donald leaned back in his seat, relaxed.

Daisy began to turn the wheel more quickly. "This is fun!" she laughed.

Donald's stomach flipped and flopped. "Uh, Daisy," he said, gulping. "This is too much for you! We should slow down!"

But Daisy was happily waving to Mickey and Minnie as they flew past, and she didn't hear Donald.

When the ride stopped, Donald stumbled out of the teacup.

"Are you okay?" Daisy asked.

Donald swallowed. "Of course!" he said, and tried to smile. "But let's do something a little slower next . . . so you stop feeling dizzy," he added hurriedly. "How about the carousel?"

Donald felt better as he hopped onto the carousel. He picked the biggest, most powerful-looking horse he could find. Daisy chose a pretty yellow pony beside him.

Donald grinned. He was sure he could make Daisy forget all about the teacups by showing her some real rodeo moves!

As the carousel started to move, Donald let go of the pole. "Look, Daisy, no hands!" he cried. Then he stood on the horse's back and waved his hat like a cowboy.

"Be careful, Donald!" Daisy cried.

Donald laughed. "Cowboys aren't careful! Watch this, Daisy! I'm going to jump onto the horse in front of me."

Donald leaped. But the carousel was slowing down. Donald flew over the horse's head and landed flat on his back.

When the ride stopped, Daisy hurried over to Donald. "Are you okay?" she asked.

"Of course I am!" Donald declared. "I'll make it next time!"

"Maybe we should try something else," Daisy said. "How about a game?"

Donald and Daisy walked to the game booths. They stopped in front of a table with a big jar of jelly beans. A sign next to the table read GUESS THE NUMBER, WIN A PRIZE.

Donald walked around the jar, examining it from every angle. Scratching his head, he muttered, "One hundred jelly beans times twenty, plus thirty, plus another two hundred seventy-three, times . . .

"I've got it!" he shouted at last. "One million, nine hundred and twenty-one thousand, and fifty-two!"

"Sorry," said the booth worker. "Try again!"

"What?" Donald cried, stomping his foot. "How could I have gotten it wrong?"

"Donald!" Daisy called from a nearby booth. "Isn't this teddy bear adorable?"

Donald raced over to the booth. If he could win the bear for Daisy, it wouldn't matter that he'd lost the jelly bean game.

Donald bought a ticket, grabbed a fishing rod, and dipped it in the water. He needed to catch a fish to win.

Donald waited and waited. Finally, he felt something tug on his line.

"Got it!" he shouted, pulling up his rod.

"You got *something*, all right," said the booth worker. "But it's not a fish!"

Donald looked down. He had caught a boot!

While Daisy went off to explore the rest of the fair, Donald looked around at the other booths. Finally, he spied a giant panda displayed at the next game. "'Test your strength,'" Donald read aloud.

He was sure he would win a prize for Daisy this time. He just needed to hit a pad with a giant mallet. If he hit it hard enough, a puck would hit a bell, and he'd win the panda!

Donald handed over his ticket and took hold of the mallet. He swung, but the puck only went halfway to the bell. He handed over another ticket and swung the mallet harder. The puck rose three-quarters of the way. Donald tried again. The puck *almost* reached the bell.

Donald had only one ticket left. This was his last chance! He raised the mallet high. But he was so tired from all the swinging that he dropped it smack on his foot.

As Donald hopped around holding his sore foot, he tripped over the fallen mallet. *CRASH!* Donald landed on the pad at the bottom of the bell tower.

The puck flew up and—*BONG!* The gong sounded. Donald won the prize!

Just then, Daisy ran over. "Donald!" she cried. "I went to the Golf-o-Rama game and got a hole in one! Here, I won this for you!"

Daisy handed Donald a giant stuffed lion.

Donald smiled. His day certainly hadn't gone the way he'd planned. But the lion *was* awfully cute.

"Come on, Daisy," Donald said, giving Daisy the panda he'd won. "Let's go home. All *four* of us!"

Mickey's Campout

Mickey Mouse and his friends were excited. It was time for their annual campout!

Everyone had an important job. Mickey packed the tents. Goofy learned how to build a fire. Minnie and Daisy made dinner. And Donald bought some new flashlights.

"Is everybody ready?" Mickey asked when they had packed up the car. "Let's go!"

Mickey drove up a mountain and through the woods. Finally, he parked the car next to a lake. "Here we are!" he said.

"Gosh, smell that fresh air!" Goofy said as he took a deep breath. "What should we do first?"

"Let's set up our tents," Mickey suggested.

"I've never put up a tent before," Minnie said.

"It's easy!" Mickey told her. "Just slip the tent poles into the pockets."

"Um, Mickey?" Daisy said. "Where are the poles?"

Mickey's eyes grew wide. "Oh, no!" he exclaimed. "I forgot them!"

"That's okay, Mickey," Goofy said. "We'll have just as much fun sleeping under the stars."

As the sun started to set, Daisy shivered. "It's getting a little chilly," she said.

"Maybe we should build a campfire," Donald suggested.

"Sure!" Goofy replied. "Let's go find some firewood."

Mickey and his friends hiked into the forest to gather some firewood. When they had enough, Goofy showed them how to pile the sticks inside a circle of rocks.

"Stand back while I light the fire, everybody," Goofy said. Then he frowned. "Uh-oh. I forgot to bring the matches!"

"Don't worry, Goofy," Minnie said. "Our sleeping bags will keep us warm. Now, who's hungry? We have hot dogs, corn—"

"And s'mores for dessert!" added Daisy.

But Minnie and Daisy found a big surprise when they reached the picnic basket: the basket had tipped over and something had eaten all the food!

"No tents, no campfire, and no dinner," grumbled Donald. "At least we have flashlights!"

Click.

Donald pushed the button on the flashlight, but it didn't shine.

Click.

He tried again. Nothing happened.

"Aw, shucks!" Donald cried. "I remembered to buy flashlights— but I forgot to buy batteries!"

Suddenly, a flash of lightning lit up the sky.

"Maybe we should just go home," Minnie said. "We can't camp in the rain without tents."

"Or dinner," added Daisy.

"Or a campfire," Goofy chimed in.

"Or a flashlight," Donald said.

Mickey agreed and the group rushed to the car.

No one spoke for the whole drive home. Mickey could tell that his friends were very disappointed.

As they walked into his house, Mickey had an idea. "I know!" he said. "Instead of having a campout, let's have a camp-in! We can camp right here in the living room."

"Oh, Mickey, what a great idea!" Minnie cried. "That sounds like so much fun!"

Mickey got the tent poles from the basement. Then he put up the tents while Goofy built a fire in the fireplace.

Meanwhile, Donald found some extra batteries. In the kitchen, Minnie and Daisy made an even better picnic dinner.

Outside, the rain kept pouring down, but Mickey and his friends didn't mind. Their tents were strong and sturdy. The fire was warm and toasty. The flashlights shined brightly. And their picnic was delicious!

Disney's MICKEY & MINNIE

Minnie's Missing Recipe

Minnie hurried up to Mickey's front door and rang the bell. "Mickey!" she said when he opened the door. "I need your help!"

"What's the matter, Minnie?" Mickey asked.

"My cinnamon swirl cake recipe is missing!" she said. "I had the recipe card this morning, but now I can't find it anywhere. And the annual baking contest is this afternoon!"

Just then, Pluto ran up the driveway. He dropped a rolled-up paper at Mickey's feet and began to bark.

"Thanks for bringing in the newspaper, Pluto!" Mickey said. "I'll read it later. Right now I have to help Minnie find her missing recipe. Come on, Minnie. Let's go!"

Mickey and Minnie hurried off to her house. Pluto picked up the paper and followed.

At Minnie's house, Mickey and Minnie searched the kitchen. The recipe card was nowhere to be found.

"When was the last time you saw it?" Mickey asked.

Minnie thought hard. "It was on the counter this morning," she said. "I had just started to bake when Donald rushed in. He wanted to show me his postcard collection."

That gave Mickey an idea. "Maybe Donald accidentally took your recipe card when he picked up his postcards," he suggested.

Pluto barked at Mickey and dropped the rolled-up paper at his feet again.

"Sorry, boy!" said Mickey. "No time to read the paper now. We've got to track down Minnie's recipe."

Over at Donald's house, Mickey and Minnie found their friend staring at his postcards. "There are five postcards missing from my collection!" Donald said sadly.

"That's funny," Mickey said. "Minnie is missing something, too."

"That's right," Minnie said. "I can't find my cinnamon swirl cake recipe."

"We were wondering," Mickey said, "do you think you might have picked it up by accident when you were at Minnie's house this morning?"

Donald shrugged and looked through his postcards. "It's not here," he said. "But maybe wherever my missing postcards are—"

"Is where my recipe card is, too!" Minnie said.

"I know I had all of my postcards when I got back from Minnie's this morning," Donald said. "I was flipping through them as I came in the door—and tripped over Huey. The boys were working on a collage in the middle of the hallway!"

Minnie gasped. "You don't think they accidentally used some postcards in their collage, do you, Donald?"

Donald knew that his nephews' collage was a project for school. So Mickey, Minnie, Donald, and Pluto went to wait for the boys at the bus stop.

"Boys," Donald said when they got off the school bus. "Did you use my postcards in your collage this morning?"

Donald's nephews blushed. They looked at each other with wide, troubled eyes. "Those were yours, Uncle Donald?" Huey asked.

"We thought they were pieces of junk mail," Dewey said with a shrug.

"Junk mail?" cried Donald angrily.

"Now, now," said Minnie calmly. "It was just an accident, Donald." Then she turned to Huey, Dewey, and Louie. "Where is the collage now?"

Louie shrugged. "It's the strangest thing," he said. "I rolled it up and put it in my backpack this morning."

"But when we got on the bus, it was gone!" Dewey finished.

"Which means . . ." said Mickey, "it must have fallen out somewhere between Donald's house and the bus stop!"

The group searched everywhere, from the bus stop all the way back to Donald's house. They even checked Mickey's and Minnie's yards. But they couldn't find the collage anywhere!

Pluto whined and dropped his rolled-up paper at Huey's feet.

Huey looked down. "Hey! This is it!" he exclaimed. "Pluto had it all along!"

The boys unrolled the paper and showed off their collage—complete with Donald's missing postcards and Minnie's recipe card.

"Aw, Pluto!" Mickey said, patting him on the head. "You were trying to help us find it the whole time!"

"Thanks, Pluto," Minnie said. "Now I can go home and bake *two* cinnamon swirl cakes: one for the contest, and one for you!"

And that's exactly what she did.

A Model Patient

Minnie Mouse dashed into Mickey's house one morning with her kitten, Figaro, and some very exciting news.

"*Pet Food Digest* is looking for models for its next issue!" she said. "Wouldn't Figaro be great?"

"He sure would!" Mickey said. "And what about Pluto? He's a natural, too! Let's send in their pictures!"

A few days later, Mickey and Minnie got letters from the magazine. Someone was coming to take pictures of Pluto and Figaro the next day!

The photo shoot started smoothly, but it didn't stay that way. "Look! Isn't he cute!" Mickey said when he saw Figaro sneaking into Pluto's picture.

But when Pluto saw that Figaro was carrying *his* chew toy, he was *not* happy!

The next thing Mickey knew, Pluto was chasing Figaro all
around the room!

Boom! Down tumbled the backdrop.

Crash! Over fell the lights.

"No, Pluto!" Mickey cried. "Bad dog!"

But Pluto just growled. He did not want Figaro playing with his
toy.

Suddenly, Pluto stopped growling. He backed up and held his paw to his nose.

"What happened, Pluto?" said Mickey. "Did Figaro scratch you?"

Pluto nodded, whining softly as Mickey gently patted his head.

"We'd better take you to the vet," Mickey said.

"You know," said the photographer, "I know a great vet. Dr. Daisy! I bet she could see you right away."

Dr. Daisy was more than happy to help Pluto. "Say, when was the last time Pluto had a checkup?" she asked as she swabbed his nose.

"Gosh," Mickey answered. "I guess it's been a while."

"Well, then, we should take care of that today, too," Dr. Daisy said.

"You know," Dr. Daisy told the photographer, "if you'd like, you can take pictures while I treat Pluto. Your readers might like to see what happens at a checkup."

The photographer and his assistant thought for a second. That wasn't what they had *planned* to photograph, but it *did* sound like a good idea!

Dr. Daisy scratched Pluto's back. "I can already tell you're going to be a good patient," she said.

Dr. Daisy looked in Pluto's ears to make sure they were nice and clean. She checked his teeth to make sure they were healthy. She even weighed him and measured his height.

By the time Dr. Daisy listened to Pluto's heart, Pluto was starting to think that getting a checkup was a lot of fun!

Then Dr. Daisy held up a needle. When Pluto saw it, he covered his head.

"Pluto's *never* liked shots," Mickey told Dr. Daisy. Suddenly, he had an idea. He knew something Pluto *did* like.

Mickey reached into his pocket and pulled out a treat. "How about a bone, Pluto?" he asked.

Pluto quickly sat up. He was so focused on the bone that he didn't even notice when Dr. Daisy gave him his shot!

A few weeks later, Minnie sat in Dr. Daisy's office reading the new issue of *Pet Food Digest*.

"This is such a good article about checkups!" Minnie said. "I never knew how important they were. Aren't you excited, Figaro? It's finally your turn!"

Fireman Goofy

One afternoon, Mickey Mouse headed to the fire station with Huey, Dewey, and Louie. They had offered to decorate an antique fire engine for the Town Day parade the next morning.

"Uncle Donald is working on a top secret parade float," said Louie. "He won't let us see it."

"Don't worry," Mickey answered. "Our engine will be the pride of the parade."

Mickey and the boys arrived just in time to see Goofy slide
down the brass pole in the middle of the fire station.

"Hiya, gang," Goofy said.

"Goofy is a junior volunteer, just like me," Mickey explained.

"It must be hard work being a firefighter," Louie said.

"It sure is," Goofy responded. "Do you remember when the hotel caught fire? We had to rescue about twenty people. I even saved Mrs. Porter's parakeet!"

"Gosh, Goofy," said Mickey. "If I remember right, the firefighters rescued the parakeet. They just gave it to you to hold."

"But I was a big help," Goofy said. "I found Mrs. Porter and gave her back her pet bird."

"I'll tell you another story, boys," Goofy said. "A couple of years ago, there was a big fire in the park. I rushed into the forest, and we saved the woods from burning to the ground!"

"I remember that night," said Mickey. "It was cold. You and I passed out blankets to the campers. I don't remember doing much else."

Goofy looked embarrassed. "Why don't we get started on the fire engine," he said, changing the subject. Mickey and the boys agreed.

While Mickey polished the engine, Goofy gathered the decorations.

Finally, the fire engine was ready. Everyone headed home. They could not wait for the parade.

The following morning, the whole town turned out to watch the parade. The boys' fire engine led the way—with Mickey at the wheel.

"We're sure to win the blue ribbon for best float," said Huey. He looked back over his shoulder. "Uncle Donald's float doesn't stand a chance!"

Donald's float was just behind the fire engine. He had mounted a spaceship on his old truck.

"Get a good look," Donald shouted to the crowd. "My float is going to send the judges to the moon!"

As Donald drove his wobbly rocket down the street, sparks flew everywhere.

Suddenly, the rocket caught fire.

Mickey pulled to a stop, and Goofy hooked one of the fire
engine's hoses to a hydrant. Then he began spraying Donald's float
with water. Before long, the fire was completely out.

Later, during the awards ceremony for best float, the mayor asked Goofy to come forward. He thanked Goofy and shook his hand. Then he gave him a medal that said HERO. Goofy smiled as the crowd cheered for him. He was a real firefighter at last!

Mickey and the Kitten-Sitters

"Guess what?" Mickey Mouse said to his nephews, Morty and Ferdie. "We're going to watch Minnie's kitten, Figaro, while she visits her cousin. Isn't that exciting?"

Before Morty and Ferdie could answer, they heard wild clucking, flapping, and crowing coming from next door. Suddenly, Pluto raced across the lawn. A big, angry rooster followed close behind him.

"Pluto!" Minnie scolded. "Chasing chickens again! Aren't you ashamed?"

Pluto *was* a bit ashamed, but only because he had let the rooster bully him.

"It's a good thing Figaro is staying with you," Minnie told Mickey as she got into her car. "Maybe he can teach Pluto how to behave!"

Minnie was hardly out of sight when Figaro leaped out of
Mickey's arms and scampered into the kitchen. With one quick hop,
he jumped onto the table and knocked over a pitcher of cream.

Pluto growled at the kitten, but Mickey just cleaned up the mess.
"Take it easy, Pluto," he said. "Figaro is our guest."

At dinnertime, Pluto ate his food the way a good dog should.
But no matter how hard Mickey and the boys tried, Figaro wouldn't
touch the special food Minnie had left for him.

At bedtime, Figaro would not use the cushion Minnie had brought for him. Instead, he got into bed with Ferdie and tickled his ears. Finally, he bounced off to the kitchen.

"Uncle Mickey," called Morty. "Did you remember to close the kitchen window?"

"Oh, no!" cried Mickey, jumping out of bed. The kitchen window was open, and Figaro was nowhere to be seen.

Mickey and the boys searched the entire house. They looked upstairs and downstairs, under every chair, and even in the yard. But they couldn't find the little kitten anywhere.

"You two stay here," Mickey told his nephews. "Pluto and I will find Figaro."

Mickey and Pluto went to Minnie's house first, but Figaro wasn't there. Next they went to the park down the street.

"Have you seen a little black-and-white kitten?" Mickey asked a policeman.

"I certainly have!" answered the policeman. "He was teasing the ducks by the pond!"

Mickey and Pluto hurried to the pond. Figaro wasn't there, but they *did* find some small, muddy footprints.

Mickey and Pluto followed the trail of footprints to Main Street, where they met a grocery truck driver.

"Have you seen a kitten?" Mickey asked.

"Have I!" cried the driver. "He knocked over my eggs!"

Mickey groaned as he paid for the eggs. Where was Figaro?

Mickey and Pluto searched the whole town, but there was no sign of the kitten. By the time they returned home, the sun was starting to rise.

Soon Minnie drove up. "Where is Figaro?" she asked.

No one answered.

"Something has happened to him!" Minnie cried. "Can't I trust
you to watch *one* sweet little kitten?"

Just then, there was a loud clucking from the yard next door. A dozen frantic hens came flapping over the fence, with Figaro close behind.

"There's your sweet little kitten!" exclaimed Mickey. "He ran away last night and teased the ducks in the park. Then he broke the eggs in the grocery truck and—"

"And now he's chasing chickens!" Minnie finished.

"I had hoped Figaro would teach Pluto some manners," Minnie said. "Instead, Pluto has been teaching him to misbehave!"

"Pluto didn't do anything wrong," Ferdie said.

But Minnie wouldn't listen. She picked up Figaro and quickly drove away.

"Don't worry, boys," said Mickey. "We'll tell her the whole story later, when she's not so upset."

"Please don't tell her too soon," begged Morty. "As long as Aunt Minnie thinks Pluto is a bad dog, we won't have to kitten-sit Figaro."

Mickey smiled and said, "Maybe we *should* wait a little while. We could all use some peace and quiet." And with that, he and Pluto settled down for a well-deserved nap.

Disney's MICKEY & MINNIE

Donald's Museum Mix-Up

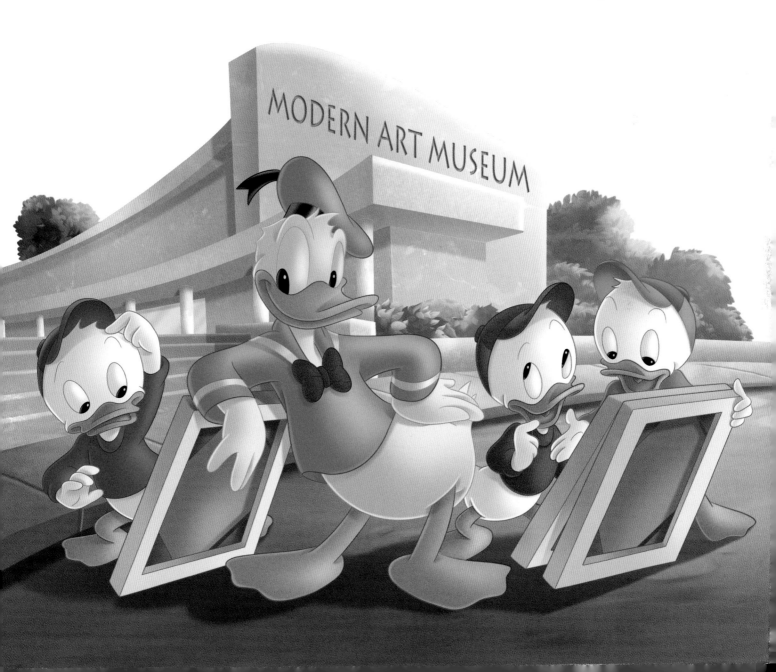

Donald Duck was home alone, reading the newspaper. His nephews were out, and Donald was enjoying the peace and quiet. Smiling widely, he turned a page. The words FAMOUS ARTIST PAOLA PIZAZZO TO ATTEND OPENING OF NEW EXHIBIT jumped out at him.

"Phooey!" Donald shouted, jumping to his feet. He had almost forgotten why the house was empty. His nephews were at the museum, taking an art class. Donald was supposed to pick them up—right then!

Donald raced to his car. In no time at all, he reached the museum. Suddenly, he remembered that he had been making tea when he ran out of the house. The water was probably boiling by now. He had to get back home, and fast!

Donald hurried through the halls to his nephews' classroom.

Huey, Dewey, and Louie were waiting inside. "Hi, Uncle Donald!"

Dewey said. "Come look at our pictures!"

"They're over there," Huey added, pointing.

Donald imagined the tea kettle whistling away at home. He didn't have time to look at the boys' art now.

Scooping up some paintings, Donald hurried his nephews out the door. At home, he laid out the paintings on the table. "Wow, these are interesting," he said.

"Yes, they are," Huey agreed.

"Who painted them?" Dewey asked.

"*What?*" Donald shouted. "Aren't these *your* pictures?"

His nephews shook their heads. "Look," Dewey said. "They're signed by someone else."

Donald peered at the corner of the first painting. The name PAOLA PIZAZZO was scrawled on the bottom. He had accidentally taken a famous artist's paintings from the museum!

Donald gulped. The museum would be setting up Paola's show soon. They were sure to notice the three missing paintings!

"We have to sneak these back," he told his nephews.

Donald and the boys raced to the car. "Remember," Donald said when they reached the museum, "no one can see us!"

Donald and his nephews crept through the museum as quietly as they could, tiptoeing past visitors and hiding from guards.

In the east wing, they pressed themselves against a mural.

In the north wing, they tried to blend in with the statues.

212

Donald and his nephews were nearing the special exhibit wing when they heard someone say, "This way. Paola's paintings will go over here."

The ducks dove under a table full of priceless vases. From beneath the table, Donald saw the museum director hurry by, followed by a group of workers carrying Paola's artwork.

Donald watched as the workers hung the paintings on the wall. Suddenly, voices rang out down the hall. The artist, Paola Pizazzo, swept past. Reporters and photographers trailed behind her. The reporters stopped in front of the paintings.

"Brilliant!" said one.

"Masterpieces!" said another.

"Do you have a favorite, Paola?" asked a third.

"Hey!" said the nephews. "Those are *our* pictures!"

"I love all my paintings equally," Paola told everyone.

"She thinks *she* painted them!" the boys whispered. "Uncle Donald, do something!"

But Donald just stared at the artist, too nervous to do anything.

"Each one is special to me in its own way," Paola continued.

"Special!" Donald sputtered. He jumped in front of the crowd. "How special can they be if you don't even know what you painted and what you didn't?"

Donald waved at the boys. "My nephews painted these pictures, not Ms. Pizazzo."

The room fell silent.

"That's impossible!" the director finally said. "Right, Ms. Pizazzo?"

Paola looked confused. "I don't see how—"

"Your paintings got mixed up with student work from the art class next door," Donald interrupted.

"We can prove it," said the boys, moving toward them. They led everyone from one painting to the next. Each one was signed FOR UNCLE DONALD.

Donald held up the other pictures. "Here are your paintings, Ms. Pizazzo."

Paola knew she had to make up for her mistake. The next day, when museum-goers arrived for Paola's opening, they saw a sign that said BRIGHT NEW ARTISTS. The boys' paintings hung beneath it. Donald smiled and waved as the museum guests looked at the art. He was proud of his nephews for having their work shown, but he was even more excited that his name was hanging in the museum. That made him famous, too. And Donald was just fine with that!

Mickey Mouse
and the Pet Show

It was a perfect day for a cookout. Mickey Mouse and his nephews, Morty and Ferdie, were preparing lunch.

Pluto barked a friendly welcome to Minnie as she joined the boys in the yard.

"I'm sorry I'm late," she said, "but I have great news. I've just been elected chairperson of the Charity Pet Show. We're raising money to build a new shelter for stray animals."

"We should enter Pluto in the show!" Morty suggested.

"Yeah! We can teach him to do tricks," said Ferdie. "Can we, Uncle Mickey? Please?"

"All right," Mickey said. "It's for a good cause."

Mickey and Minnie watched as the boys started to train Pluto.

"Roll over, Pluto," Morty said.

But Pluto just sat up and wagged his tail.

"Maybe we should show him what we want him to do," said Ferdie.

Pluto watched, puzzled, as both boys rolled over in the grass.

"Let's try something that *he* likes to do," suggested Morty.

Ferdie ordered Pluto to lie down, but Pluto jumped up and began chasing his tail instead.

All week long, Morty and Ferdie tried to teach Pluto new tricks. He fetched, rolled over, lay down, begged, and shook hands . . . but only when *he* wanted to.

"Well, he *is* doing tricks," said Mickey.

"They're just not the *right* tricks," said Ferdie.

"He'll never win first prize," said Morty.

On the day of the show, Mickey and the boys took Pluto to the empty lot next door, where the show was being held. Minnie sold Mickey three tickets, then pointed happily to the cashbox.

"We've made enough to pay for the new animal shelter!" she told him.

"That's great!" cried Mickey.

What *wasn't* great was Pluto's performance.

He shook hands when he was told to sit. He rolled over when he should have jumped. He barked when he was supposed to lie down. Worst of all, when Police Chief O'Hara was choosing Best Pet of the Day, Pluto growled at him! The chief didn't know it, but he was standing right where Pluto had buried his bone!

Suddenly, the crowd heard a scream from the ticket booth.

"Help! Stop, thief! Help!"

"That's Minnie!" Mickey gasped.

"The ticket money!" Morty and Ferdie shouted.

Mickey, the boys, and Chief O'Hara ran to the booth.

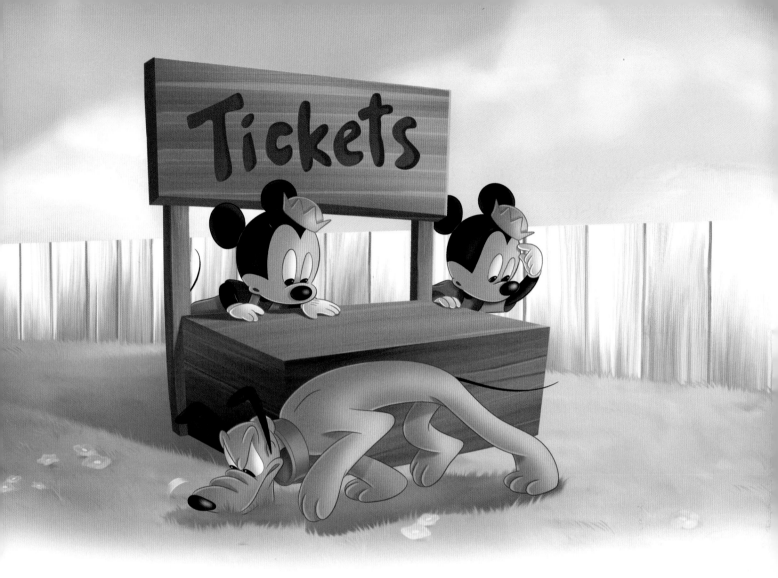

Pluto was already at the scene of the crime. He was busily
sniffing around.

"All the money is gone," Minnie said. "I walked away for one
minute. When I came back, I saw someone running away with the
cashbox."

"What did the robber look like?" asked the chief.

Before Minnie could answer, Pluto took off. A moment later, the thief ran screaming out of the woods. He was holding on to the cashbox—and Pluto was holding on to him! Pluto growled and tugged on the thief's suspenders.

Snap! The thief's suspenders broke and shot him right into the arms of Chief O'Hara.

Later that afternoon, Chief O'Hara presented Pluto with the Four-Footed Hero medal.

The chief smiled and said, "Thanks to Pluto, every animal will have a place to go—and a chance to find a good home."

At home, Pluto waited by the front door.

"You know," said Morty, "I don't care if Pluto isn't a show dog. He's something better. He's a *hero* dog."

Mickey, Minnie, and Ferdie agreed. Then, without being told, Pluto shook hands with everyone, because this time *he* wanted to.

Goofy's Kite Contest

Mickey held his jacket closed. He had been out for a walk when the wind kicked up. Now he was cold!

Mickey looked around. Goofy lived nearby. Maybe Mickey could warm up at his house.

Mickey rang the doorbell. Inside, he heard a rustling sound.

"Oh, hi, Mickey!" Goofy said, letting Mickey inside. There was a newspaper tucked under his arm. "Look at this!"

Goofy held out the newspaper and pointed.

"'Kite contest,'" Mickey read out loud.

"Can you believe it?" Goofy said. "The contest is in one week. Whoever flies their kite the highest wins a prize!"

"Gosh," Mickey said. "That sounds like fun."

Goofy grinned. "I'm going to build the highest-flyingest kite you've ever seen," he said. "Do you want to help?"

Mickey laughed. "You bet!"

The two friends set to work building kites. But what kind would fly the highest? A small, light kite? A big, heavy kite? Should the kite be made of paper? What kind of string should they use?

Mickey and Goofy tried everything. Finally, they were ready to take their kites to the park.

Goofy and Mickey tested kite after kite. Their little blue kite flew high, but its tail broke in the strong wind. Their dragonfly kite was pretty, but it was hard to steer.

Finally, Goofy found a kite to fly in the contest. It was the biggest kite they'd made. The string was thick and strong, and the kite was more than ten feet tall!

On the day of the contest, Mickey helped Goofy take his kite to the park. It was so big it would not fit in the car!

When they reached the park, they saw lots of kites. Some of them looked like dragons. Some of them looked like paper boxes. There were bright colors and long, shining ribbons everywhere.

Before long, kites filled the air. Goofy's kite tugged hard at the string. He let more and more string slip through his fingers. Soon his kite was higher than anyone else's!

"You're doing it, Goofy!" Mickey cried. "You're winning!"

Goofy grinned. His kite was nearly at the end of its string!

Just then, a big gust of wind blew.

Goofy's kite flew even higher. The spool jerked in his hands, but he held on tight.

Goofy's kite soared up and up. Goofy dug his heels into the ground, but it was no good! The kite was too strong. Hanging on to the spool, he rose into the air!

"Mickey!" Goofy yelled. "What do I do?"

"Don't let go!" Mickey shouted. His voice sounded far away.

Goofy looked down. He was very high up, and Mickey looked very small!

"Oh, boy," Goofy said. He was scared, but flying so high was kind of exciting!

Goofy wiggled around. Soon the kite string was tied tightly around his waist.

Hanging from his kite, Goofy flew through the air. Beneath him, the town swept by.

"There's Donald!" he said. "And there's Minnie!"

Goofy shouted and waved to his friends, but he was too high! They didn't see him.

"I wonder where this kite is going," Goofy said.

Suddenly, Goofy heard a voice cry, "Hang in there, Goofy!"

He looked around. Who was shouting at him?

It was Mickey! He was following the kite in his car.

Mickey pointed at something in the distance. "Try to land on that hill!" he yelled.

Goofy nodded. He untied the string around his waist and got ready to land.

As Goofy's feet hit the ground, he let go of the string. The kite flew away.

Mickey parked the car and ran over.

"Gee, Goofy," he said. "You won the contest, but you lost your kite."

"That's okay, Mickey," Goofy said. "I don't think I'm going to be flying any more kites for a while."

"I bet!" Mickey agreed.

"Yeah," Goofy said. "I'm going to learn how to fly airplanes instead!"

Donald Duck
and the Dairy Farm

Early one summer morning, Mickey Mouse, Donald Duck, and Donald's nephews arrived at Grandma Duck's farm. They had promised to take care of Grandma's cows while she was on vacation.

Mickey and the boys found the cows drinking from a pond.
Mickey, Huey, Dewey, and Louie brought them into the barn. But
one cow would not move. She was standing behind a big, round
bale of hay.

"Here, cow! Here, cow!" Donald called.

Mickey and the boys hurried over to see what was happening. Next to the cow stood a little calf.

"This must be Rosie and her new calf!" Mickey said. "We're supposed to take the calf to the barn and help it drink from a bottle."

Donald tried to lead the calf to the barn, but Rosie blocked his way. He tried to push Rosie aside, but she pushed him back. Soon Rosie was chasing Donald around the pasture.

Meanwhile, Mickey, Huey, Dewey, and Louie led the calf inside and fed it.

Suddenly, Donald dashed into a milking stall, with Rosie close behind him. Donald slipped away from the cow, slammed the stall door shut, and leaned against it.

"Guess I showed her who's boss!" he said, wiping his forehead.

Donald watched as Mickey and the boys hooked the other cows to the milking machines.

"That looks easy," he said. But when he tried it with Rosie, she pushed him over and started to run. "Whoa!" Donald shouted, grabbing her tail.

As Rosie dragged Donald through the barn, his feet got tangled in the hoses that carried milk to the storage tank.

Snap! One of the hoses came loose.

Milk sprayed everywhere, soaking Donald from head to toe and splashing in his eyes.

Donald stumbled over hoses and milk cans and bumped into doors. Finally, he put his foot straight into a bucket, tripped, and fell into a feed bin.

"Oof!" Donald gasped as he climbed out covered with bits of mashed grain. "That's it!"

Donald grabbed an old milking stool and
a bucket and marched toward Rosie.

"I'm going to milk this cow the old-fashioned
way—by hand!"

When Rosie saw Donald approaching, a sly glint came into her eyes. As soon as he got close enough, she gave him a powerful kick and sent him flying through the air.

Splash! Donald landed headfirst in a full can of milk.

Mickey pulled Donald out of the can. "I think you've helped enough for today," he said. "We'll finish milking Rosie."

Mickey calmly milked the cow, and then the boys put her in a stall with her calf. After their chores were done, the gang trooped back to the house for a rest.

264

Just then, Grandma Duck drove up. "I missed my cows too much to go away," she said.

"Hmph! I hope I never see another cow again," Donald said.

"Hmmm," Grandma said, handing out gifts to everyone. "That's too bad."

Mickey opened his box, and everyone began to laugh—even Donald. Inside was a huge piece of chocolate, and it was shaped just like a cow!

Minnie's Secret Scavenger Hunt

One beautiful spring morning, Minnie woke up to find a surprise waiting for her. Someone had slipped an envelope under her front door!

"What could this be, Figaro?" Minnie asked. She opened the envelope and pulled out a note:

Welcome to the Secret Scavenger Hunt! To win your prize, collect all the items below and bring them to the park by one o'clock. And remember—it's a secret!

"Let's see," Minnie said as she looked at the list. "Item number one: a picnic blanket. That's easy!"

Minnie opened the closet and pulled out a soft blanket. She also took out a large basket.

"I can use this to carry everything," she said.

Then, placing the blanket in the basket, Minnie waved good-bye to Figaro and headed outside. This was going to be fun!

"Item number two: three cucumbers," Minnie read. "Oh, I do hope my cucumbers are ready to be picked!"

Minnie went to her garden. Sure enough, several of the big green vegetables were ready to be eaten. *What perfect timing!* Minnie thought. Then she plucked the three biggest cucumbers from the vine and added them to her basket.

Minnie was headed for the woods when she saw Goofy coming her way. She quickly hid her basket.

"Oh, hi, Minnie," Goofy said. "What are you doing out here?"

Minnie was about to answer when she noticed that Goofy was hiding some blueberries behind his back. Maybe he was part of the scavenger hunt, too!

"I'm just out for a walk. I'll see you later, Goofy!" Minnie replied. Then the two friends rushed off in different directions.

Minnie continued into the woods. Soon she had found the third item on her list: a stick as tall as she was.

But as Minnie looked around, she realized she was lost. She had wandered too far looking for the stick.

Minnie decided to keep walking. Soon she heard a bubbling noise. "It's a stream!" she said. Nearby was a patch of green plants with red peeking out from underneath. Minnie bent down to examine them.

"Strawberries!" she exclaimed. "These are the next item on my list: fifteen strawberries."

Minnie picked the sweet fruits and added them to her basket.

Minnie looked at the next item on her list: five smooth stones. "The brook is a great place to find smooth stones!" she said.

Minnie left her basket on the shore and waded into the water. In no time she had found five smooth rocks on the streambed.

Minnie had found two more scavenger hunt items, but she was still lost. She tried to walk in one direction for a while, but somehow she just ended up back at the brook.

"Oh, no!" she said. "It's almost one o'clock, and I don't know how to get out of the woods. I'll never finish the Secret Scavenger Hunt if I don't find the path soon."

Suddenly, Minnie spotted something on the ground.

"Blueberries! Goofy was picking these. Some must have fallen out of his basket," Minnie realized. "If I follow them, they should lead me back to the path and out of the woods!"

Minnie followed the trail until, finally, she found the path—and a patch of daffodils!

"A yellow flower!" Minnie cried. "That's the last item on my list!"

Minnie picked one of the flowers and added it to her basket. Then she happily skipped down the path. When she reached the park, Minnie saw her friends arriving with their own baskets.

"Surprise!" Mickey called. "Congratulations on finishing the Secret Scavenger Hunt! I left each of you a list of items to collect. Now we can combine them and have a springtime party!"

Minnie smiled as she and her friends got to work.
She laid down her picnic blanket. Donald tied balloons to a nearby
tree. Daisy got out a vase, and the friends all added the flowers
they had picked. Finally, Mickey cut up the berries and vegetables
for a delicious lunch.

The five friends played in the park for the rest of the afternoon. Donald used Minnie's stick to hit the piñata Mickey had brought. Minnie and Daisy played hopscotch with Minnie's stones and Daisy's chalk. And Goofy made a funny hat from Donald's newspaper. It was a wonderful party and the perfect spring day!

Chef Mickey

Mickey was excited. He was cooking a romantic dinner for Minnie. He wanted everything to be perfect. There was just one problem. . . . Mickey didn't know what to make!

Maybe my friends will have some ideas, Mickey thought.

Mickey called Donald and Goofy. The friends agreed to come over and help.

Soon Donald and Goofy arrived. They had brought Daisy to help, too!

"What should I make?" Mickey asked his friends.

"Hmmm . . . Minnie likes lasagna," said Daisy.

Daisy was right. Minnie *loved* lasagna. Mickey nodded and started to gather the ingredients.

But Donald had a different idea. "You should make a turkey,"
he said. "It's Minnie's favorite. That will show her how well you
know her!"

"How about a salad?" Goofy added.

Mickey was confused. Daisy was right, but Donald was right,
too. And a salad *did* sound good. What was he going to do?

Mickey looked at the ingredients he had taken out. What if he chose wrong?

"What do you think I should do, Pluto?" he asked.

"Woof, woof," Pluto barked.

"You're right," Mickey said. "I *should* make them all!"

Soon Mickey was busy making turkey *and* lasagna *and* salad. It was a lot of food, but he was sure Minnie would love it!

Mickey looked at the clock. It was getting late! He still needed to set the table, but he was too busy cooking.

"I can help you, Mickey," Daisy said.

Daisy pulled out plates and glasses. Then she set the table, decorating it in all Minnie's favorite colors.

Meanwhile, Goofy prepared a special fruit punch.

"Gawrsh, this is fun!" he said, spilling punch all over the table as he stirred.

Finally, the drink was ready. Goofy picked up the punch bowl and headed to the dining room. He didn't see Donald walking by with the salad.

CRASH!

Goofy and Donald smacked into each other. Salad flew into the air. Punch spilled all over the floor. And Goofy fell into Daisy's beautiful table.

Hearing all the noise, Mickey raced into the dining room. He could barely believe his eyes. Everyone's hard work was ruined!

"I'm sorry, Mickey," Goofy said. "I didn't mean to ruin everything. I just wanted to help."

"Me too," Donald said. "I wanted everything to be perfect!"

Mickey looked at his sad friends. "It's okay," he said. "I know it was an accident."

With his friends' help, Mickey began to clean up the mess.

Suddenly, he sniffed the air. "Does anyone smell something burning?" Mickey asked.

Mickey opened the oven. He had been so busy cleaning that he had forgotten all about the food. Everything was overcooked!

The dining room was still a mess, and now the food was ruined, too. What was Mickey going to do?

Just then, Minnie walked through the door. "Hi, Mickey," she called sweetly. "I'm here for our special night."

Minnie looked around the messy room. Mickey was holding a burned turkey, her friends were covered in food, and the table was a mess!

"Oh, Mickey. What happened?" Minnie asked.

"I had everything planned out," Mickey told Minnie. "I wanted our night to be special, so I made all of your favorite dishes. Turkey, lasagna, and salad. I even asked Goofy and Donald to help out. But then Goofy dropped the punch, and Donald dropped the salad. After that, I guess things just got out of control."

"It's okay, Mickey," Minnie said. "I love that you wanted everything to be perfect, but that's not what's important. What's important is the time we spend together."

"Aw, shucks, Minnie," Mickey said. "Thanks! But what are we going to do about dinner?"

Minnie smiled. "I have an idea," she said.

Mickey looked at Minnie and smiled. His night wasn't what he had expected, but he was still having fun. And he had learned an important lesson. As long as he was with Minnie, nothing else mattered.

Mickey handed Minnie a slice of pizza. "You're right, Minnie," he said. "This *is* the perfect night after all."